Oisín and
Tír na nÓg

This story was adapted by author Ann Carroll
and illustrated by Derry Dillon

Published 2013
by: In a Nutshell
an imprint of Poolbeg Press Ltd

123 Grange Hill, Baldoyle
Dublin 13, Ireland

Text © Poolbeg Press Ltd 2013

1

ISBN 978 1 84223 605 5

Cover design and illustrations by Derry Dillon
Printed by GPS Colour Graphics Ltd, Alexander Road, Belfast BT6 9HP

This book belongs to

Tír na nÓg

Also in the Nutshell series

Long, long ago in Ireland, when this story began, Oisín spent the day on the seashore with the Fianna, a band of warriors led by his father, Fionn Mac Cumhaill. They were famous for their strength and bravery, and none more so than Oisín. On this day, testing his skills against the rest, he was the fastest on horseback, strongest at wrestling, best with spear and javelin. And by sunset he was still full of energy.

How wonderful it is to be young, he thought. How sad that youth can't last forever!

His father was looking tired and old. Fionn was once the greatest warrior of all; now he was heading for home and sleep.

Turning his horse, Oisín caught up on Fionn
and the rest followed. He shouted to his dogs,
"Bran, Sceolain! Home!" Together the warriors
galloped along the shore.

"Look! Oisín, look! On the waves!" one of the
warriors called.

From far out on the red-gold sea came a girl on
horseback. Amazed, they stopped.

"She's beautiful," Oisín said, enchanted by her golden hair and bright blue eyes.

"She'll bring no luck," Fionn said. As a boy he had tasted the Salmon of Knowledge and could see into the future. "Let's go now!"

But Oisín was watching the girl gallop closer. His father sighed. So much heartache lay ahead.

It's good to be old, he thought. At least I won't live to see his sorrows.

"Oisín!" the girl called, stopping her white horse before him. "I am Niamh Chinn Óir and I've come from Tír na nÓg to take you back with me." Niamh Chinn Óir meant 'Niamh of the Golden Hair'.

His friends gasped. Tír na nÓg was a magical place beyond the seas where no one ever grew old. They envied Oisín. But Fionn's heart sank.

"In the Land of Youth you'll always be as strong and handsome as you are today," Niamh continued. "There will be music and feasting, stories and contests, the best of horses and hounds, great castles to live in, as much gold and silver as you could wish for."

"And you?" Oisín asked. "Will you be with me?"

Niamh smiled. "We'll be young together for always."

And so, in spite of his father's sadness, Oisín left with Niamh on her great white horse and they galloped back across the sea.

It was just as Niamh promised. In Tír na nÓg it was always perfect summer. Everyone was young. There was no sickness or death. He loved Niamh and she loved him. She was beautiful beyond compare.

And yet . . . and yet . . .

Before long he found he missed home. He missed the seasons, the countryside, his friends. He missed his dogs, Bran and Sceolan, and the chat around the camp fire. Most of all he missed his father. If only we could talk once again, he thought.

But Niamh didn't want him to leave. "I can't go with you for I can't live where humans live. But I'll take you to the Island of Music and Merriment. There you'll be happy again."

And because he loved her, Oisín agreed to go. The music on this island cheered his heart and he was merry, until the day Niamh asked him to sing. His song was about the Fianna and the battles they'd fought. It was about bravery and friendship and it made him sad.

"I must go back," he told Niamh. "I must see them once again."

"We'll go to The Island of Victories," Niamh told him. "And there you can fight to your heart's content. It's the battles you miss, Oisín, not the warriors."

And because he didn't wish to leave her, Oisín agreed.

He fought many battles on that island, alongside great warriors. But although the fights were fierce, once Oisín realised he couldn't lose, they were meaningless. All the old sorrows returned.

"There's no point to this," he told Niamh. "No point at all. I can't forget home, or the Fianna or my father. I must go back."

"You're just weary," Niamh said, "and you will forget if we go to the Island of Sleep."

And again, Oisín agreed.

On the Island of Sleep they found a sheltered cove with white sand where the breeze brushed the waves, and Oisín fell into a slumber. But sleep brought no forgetfulness. Dreams of the Fianna crowded his mind. In one he heard his father ask, "Which of these islands, Oisín, is the Island of Happiness?"

Then he awoke, his heart full of misery. Niamh could not bear his sadness and told him, "Go! But if you do, you may not be able to come back."

"I will come back!" Oisín vowed. "All I want is to see my old friends again, to watch Bran and Sceolain race through the woods, to talk with Fionn once more and to see the land where I grew up. Less than a day, Niamh, will satisfy me. After that I'll return."

Niamh said, "Then you must let my horse carry you and you must promise not to set foot on the ground of your homeland. If you do, you'll never come back!"

Oisín promised and, because she loved him, Niamh let him go. As she watched him gallop across the waves she thought: What good is eternal youth if it brings eternal sorrow?

It seemed to Oisín only a few years had passed since he'd left home and that he'd spent only a short time on each magical island. He expected everything at home to be the same, and at first when he rode ashore he thought it was. The mountains hadn't changed, nor had the long shoreline. But as he galloped inland he saw

small stone buildings he didn't recognise. They had crosses on them. When he heard a bell peal from one of the buildings he stopped and watched, stunned, as people flocked towards it.

What had happened to everyone? They were so small! A curse must have fallen on them. They too stopped to stare at him and he galloped away.

But soon he saw other groups and noted that no man was as tall or strong as any in the Fianna. Where were his comrades? He could not find them in the old places. Indeed, the woods and fields where they'd hunted and camped were gone, villages and farmland in their place.

Then he came across six men at the edge of a meadow. They were trying to lift a huge rock and he stopped to ask if they knew where the Fianna were.

"The Fianna?" One of the men stepped towards him. "They're long gone!"

"I can see that!" Oisín was impatient. "Just tell me where they've gone and I'll be on my way."

"To their graves," the man said. "The last of the Fianna died three hundred years ago."

For a while Oisín couldn't speak with sorrow and his mind struggled to understand. Time mustn't exist in Tír na nÓg, he thought. How could I

believe only a short time had passed there? I've been away at least three centuries!

Silently he brooded and the man went back to helping the others lift the rock. But the rock wouldn't budge.

This is a different world! Oisín thought. I must get back to Niamh. There's nothing here for me.

But first he would help the men – a simple task.

"Where do you want to put that stone?"

"Stone?" They looked at each other before answering. "At the edge of the sea," they said. "But it's impossible to move!"

Oisin leaned down from the horse, lifted the huge rock with one hand and flung it far away to the edge of the sea. But the saddle had slipped around with him, the straps broke and he tumbled to the ground.

The great horse turned at once and galloped away.

Mouths open the men watched as the handsome young warrior changed instantly. His hair turned grey and wispy and a thousand wrinkles creased his face. They could see the bones beneath his skin and stepped back, horrified.

Oisín tried to stand and as they watched his efforts the men felt great pity.

"He is so old," one said.

"He needs help. We'll take him to Patrick."

Patrick was the man who'd brought Christianity to Ireland. The men gently carried Oisín to his church, where he was made comfortable.

Over the next few days Patrick listened to his story. In turn he told him about God and Heaven.

Oisín was curious. "If I become a Christian will I go to this Heaven?" he asked.

"You will."

"What's Heaven like?"

"A place where there is no more sickness and no more death and it's always summer."

"And will my dogs, Bran and Sceolain, be there?"

"Certainly not. Dogs have no souls."

"What about Fionn? And the Fianna? Will they be there."

"They were pagans, not Christians. No, they won't be there!"

Oisín thought for a while then said, "Heaven sounds just like Tír na nÓg. It's not for me. When the Fianna die, they go to the House of the Fianna in the Otherworld. That's where I'll go. My dogs will be glad to see me. Fionn and my friends will be there, impatient to tell me all that's happened. Maybe I'll see Niamh too, for I think she could live in such a place."

Patrick saw there was no changing his mind and spoke no more of Heaven.

So Oisín spent the short time that remained to him dreaming of the House of the Fianna where all those he loved would be waiting for him.

The End

Word Sounds

(Opinions may differ regarding pronunciation)

Words	Sounds
Oisín	Usheen
Tír na nÓg	Teer na nogue (nogue rhymes with rogue)
Fianna	Fee-anna
Fionn	Fee-un
Mac	Mock
Cumhaill	Cool
Sceolain	Skeogh lan (Sceo rhymes with Keogh)
Niamh	Neeve

Also available from the IN A NUTSHELL series

All you need to know about Ireland's best loved stories in a nutshell

The Story of Newgrange

Available Now!

The Salmon of Knowledge

Available Now!

The Story of Saint Patrick

Available Now!

How Cúchulainn Got His Name

Available Now!

The Children of Lir

Available Now!

The Story of The Giant's Causeway

Available Now!

Granuaile The Pirate Queen

Available Now!